THE MYSTERY OF THE GRAND BAZAAR

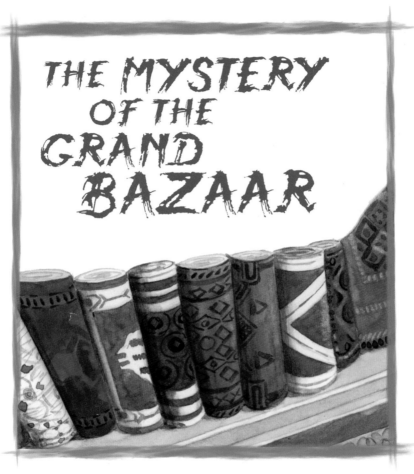

Lee Aucoin, *Creative Director*
Jamey Acosta, *Senior Editor*
Heidi Fiedler, *Editor*
Produced and designed by
Denise Ryan & Associates
Illustration © Gershom Griffith
Rachelle Cracchiolo, *Publisher*

Teacher Created Materials

5301 Oceanus Drive
Huntington Beach, CA 92649-1030
http://www.tcmpub.com
Paperback: ISBN: 978-1-4333-5645-2
Library Binding: ISBN: 978-1-4807-1744-2
© 2014 Teacher Created Materials

WRITTEN BY

...ORE

...BY

GRIFFITH

Contents

Chapter One

ZEYD FINDS BAHIR

The streets of the Grand Bazaar in Istanbul were packed with colorful stalls and busy people. The air was filled with delicious smells coming from the food stands. The streets were alive with the noise of merchants calling out to passersby.

Among the hustle and bustle, a young man named Zeyd was racing through the Bazaar. He darted nimbly through the crowds at the market. He had a job to do.

Zeyd skipped between pots and jumped over sleeping dogs. He ran through the furniture market. The whole time, he held tightly onto a delivery until he stopped outside a rug stall. "Here you are, Akel," said Zeyd breathlessly. "The delivery from the food market."

"Thank you, Zeyd!" replied Akel. "Come join me for flatbread!"

Every day, Zeyd helped the merchants of the Bazaar. He would run from one end to the other, through all sixty-four streets, collecting packages or trading goods. In return, Zeyd would receive breakfast, lunch, and supper. Sometimes, he was even given blankets or clothing.

Once, a kind merchant gave him a precious jewel! But since Zeyd saw no point in trinkets, he traded the jewel for some of his favorite pastry, *baklava*.

Zeyd said goodbye to Akel after they had shared their meal. He began to walk to the Street of Jewels. The jewel merchants often needed his help, as they trusted Zeyd.

Suddenly, Zeyd noticed something strange—a stack of rugs was moving mysteriously. Zeyd looked more closely. It was Bahir the monkey, rummaging about.

Chapter Two

SILENCE IN THE STREETS

Bahir belonged to one of the jewelers on the other side of the Bazaar.

"Are you lost, Bahir?" Zeyd bent down, and Bahir leapt onto his shoulder. Together, they walked toward the Street of Jewels.

When they arrived, a man wearing expensive garments raced up to them. It was Jorim, the powerful jewelry merchant.

"Bahir! There you are, you silly monkey!" Bahir leapt into Jorim's arms. "Thank you, young Zeyd. Where did you find him? He went running off after a chicken this morning, and I hadn't seen him since."

Zeyd laughed. Jorim offered him a gold coin, but Zeyd shook his head. He told Jorim to think nothing of it. Coins meant nothing to him.

Zeyd went home to his little room above one of the market stands. It was comfortable and a perfect size.

In the morning, Zeyd woke at his usual time. But after a few moments, he realized something was different. It was silent. Zeyd wondered why he couldn't hear merchants chatting, children playing, or donkeys braying.

Quickly, he ran downstairs into the Bazaar. It was deserted. Everything was quiet, the stalls were closed, and no one was in the streets. It wasn't until he got to the Street of Food that he could see a throng.

Zeyd pushed through the crowd to see what was going on.

Chapter Three

Jorim was standing at the front. "Who among us is a thief?" he boomed above the hubbub of merchants. "Last night, someone stole from Akel, the rug merchant. Until the thief confesses, the Bazaar will remain closed!"

The merchants surrounding him were angry. No one had ever stolen from the Bazaar before. The eighteen gates of the market closed at dusk, and guards watched over the marketplace night and day. How could anyone have stolen anything from Akel?

Zeyd spotted Akel among the crowd and asked him what had been stolen. "A bag of gold coins," Akel replied.

Zeyd was puzzled. *Why such a fuss over coins? What did gold matter when you could get all you needed by delivering packages?* He nodded and wandered through the angry crowd.

He saw that one by one, the merchants were going into a chamber to be questioned by Jorim about what they had done the day before. Zeyd watched impatiently. He just wanted the Bazaar to get back to normal.

"YOUNG MAN!" Jorim's voice boomed through the street, "Come!" Startled, Zeyd entered the chamber.

"Sit!" ordered Jorim. Zeyd sat.

"You must answer Akel's questions truthfully," said Jorim.

"Yes, Jorim," Zeyd said.

"Where were you last night, Zeyd?" Akel asked.

"Well, after I finished my deliveries, I had supper with you. Then, I went to see Jorim."

"Oh yes...of course," replied Akel. "What did you do after that?"

"I went home."

"Was anyone with you?" Akel asked.

"No," replied Zeyd.

"Did anyone see you go home?" Akel asked.

What does it matter? thought Zeyd. He was tired. He didn't know who had taken the gold.

Chapter Four

BAHIR'S SECRET STASH

After fifteen minutes of questioning, Zeyd was allowed to leave. Feeling upset by the accusations, he decided to go home. But his belly was rumbling as he dawdled through the empty streets. With the Bazaar closed, he couldn't run errands for food. Zeyd had to fix this situation quickly. Otherwise, he wouldn't be sharing flatbread for a long time!

Suddenly, Bahir caught his eye darting across the street. "Bahir! What are you doing?" Zeyd called, raising an eyebrow. Bahir picked up a button off the ground and, with a squeak, he hopped down the street toward the rug stalls.

Something clicked in Zeyd's head. What had Bahir been doing in the rugs yesterday? Curious, Zeyd followed the little monkey.

Bahir scampered to the Street of Carpets. Then, Zeyd saw Bahir's tail disappear under a pile of rugs. When Zeyd tugged at the rugs, he found a little cave Bahir had created. Inside were a few shiny buttons, an old apple core, and Akel's bag of gold coins!

Zeyd rejoiced as he grabbed Akel's bag. He called Bahir to his shoulder. He could smell a meal coming his way.

He ran the fastest he had ever run through the streets. Finally, he reached the dispersing crowd, which was starting to leave. Jorim was beginning to give up hope of finding the thief. Akel looked very sad.